THIS WALKER BOOK BELONGS TO:

For Philippa, who likes letters
H.C.

First published 1999 by Walker Books Ltd
87 Vauxhall Walk, London SE11 5HJ

This edition published 2004

2 4 6 8 10 9 7 5 3 1

Text © 1999 Joyce Dunbar
Illustrations © 1999, 2004 Helen Craig Ltd

The right of Joyce Dunbar and Helen Craig to be identified
as author and illustrator respectively of this work has been
asserted by them in accordance with the Copyright,
Designs and Patents Act 1988

This book has been typeset in Alpha

Printed in China

British Library Cataloguing in Publication Data:
a catalogue record for this book is
available from the British Library

ISBN 0-7445-6390-9

www.walkerbooks.co.uk

PaNDa and Gander

The Secret Friend

Joyce Dunbar illustrated by Helen Craig

WALKER BOOKS
AND SUBSIDIARIES
LONDON • BOSTON • SYDNEY • AUCKLAND

"Today I am going to write a thank you letter," said Gander.

"Who to?" asked Panda.

"My friend," said Gander.

"Which friend?" asked Panda.

"My secret friend," said Gander.

"I didn't know you had a secret friend,"
said Panda.

"Well I have," said Gander,
"for a while."

"What are you going to thank your
secret friend for?" asked Panda.

"I don't know yet," said Gander.

Gander started to write.

Dear secret friend,

Thank you for —

...and then he stopped.

He needed to have a good think.

He sat at his desk – and thought.

He sharpened his pencil – and thought

some more.

He went for a walk and thought all
the thoughts he could think of.
Then he had an idea.

Dear secret friend,
    Thank you for being my friend.
    Gander.

"There, I have finished my letter," he said
to Panda.

"Is that it?" asked Panda.

"Yes," said Gander,

"that's it."

"Your secret friend won't like it,"
said Panda.

"Why not?" asked Gander.

"Because you haven't finished it off
properly. You've just put 'Gander'.
'Gander' isn't enough."

"What should I put?" asked Gander.

"That depends," said Panda.

"What on?" asked Gander.

"How much you care about your
secret friend," said Panda.

"A lot," said Gander.

"Well, maybe you should put,
'Best wishes, Gander'."

"Oh, I care about him more than that,"
said Gander.

"You do?" said Panda.

"I do," said Gander.

"Then you could put, 'Love, Gander'," said Panda.

So Gander put

Love, Gander.

"Or you could put, 'Lots of love, Gander'," said Panda.

So Gander crossed out Love, Gander and put

Lots of love, Gander.

"Or you could put 'Lots and lots of love,
Gander'," said Panda.

So Gander put Lots and in front of

Lots of love,

Gander.

"What else could I put?" asked Gander.

"Three Kisses," said Panda.

So Gander put three Kisses.

"And a big red heart," said Panda.

So Gander put a big red heart.

"Now that's enough," said Panda.

"I think I shall stick some stickers on it as well," said Gander.

He stuck on a star sticker and a dinosaur sticker and a monster sticker and a spaceship sticker.

"That's definitely enough," said Panda.

"I think I shall draw a picture as well
and put a pattern all round the edges,"
said Gander.

And Gander drew a duck holding a
bunch of balloons and made a pattern
all around the edges.

"There," he said when he had finished.
"Now I think that's enough. Now I can
post my letter."
"To your secret friend," said Panda.
"That's right," answered Gander.

"And your secret friend might answer
  your letter," said Panda.

"That's right."

"Or he might not," said Panda.

"I'm sure he will," said Gander.

"But he might not do a row of kisses,"
  said Panda. "He might not draw a big
  red heart. He might not put stickers
  or do a drawing or make a
  pattern.

He might not even put
'Lots and lots of love'.
He might just
put 'Your Secret
Friend'."

"Well I shall post it all the same,"
said Gander.

"See if I care," said Panda.

Gander went to post his letter.

He made a slot in a shoebox and put
the letter in the slot.

Then he went back to see Panda.

Panda was sitting in a sulk.

"What's the matter, Panda?" asked Gander.

Panda just sulked.

"There's a letter arrived in the mailbox.

Do you want to see who it's for?"

Panda just went on sulking.

"I'll go and see," said Gander.
Gander opened the mailbox and
took out the letter.
"Well I never!" he said. "This looks
like the one I just posted!
It didn't take long
to arrive.

Look what it says on the envelope

TO MY DEAR
SECRET FRIEND,
PANDA!"

WALKER BOOKS is the world's leading
independent publisher of children's books.
Working with the best authors and illustrators
we create books for all ages, from babies
to teenagers – books your child will
grow up with and always remember. So…

FOR THE BEST CHILDREN'S BOOKS,
LOOK FOR THE BEAR